THE UPSIDE DOWN CHRISTMAS TREE

CHARLES R. ESTHER

Illustrated By: Joshua Allen

AuthorHouse™
1663 Liberty Drive
Bloomington, IN 47403
www.authorhouse.com
Phone: 1-800-839-8640

Published by AuthorHouse 07/16/2014

ISBN: 978-1-4969-2121-5 (sc)
ISBN: 978-1-4969-2122-2 (e)

Library of Congress Control Number: 2014912754

Any people depicted in stock imagery provided by Thinkstock are models,
and such images are being used for illustrative purposes only.
Certain stock imagery © Thinkstock.

This book is printed on acid-free paper.

THE UPSIDE DOWN CHRISTMAS TREE

Christmas is coming,
Let the excitement begin,
With peace on earth,
And glad tidings to men.

And none is more excited,
Than a little girl named Ann,
Oh, how she loves Christmas!
As much as any girl can.

One day Ann was shopping,
Her Mom was there too,
To buy a gift for her Dad,
And a scarf for Aunt Lou.

Ann spent her own money,
Buying markers and such,
For kids from poor families,
Who don't have very much.

4

With her Mom, Ann had lunch,
It was cheeseburgers and fries,
Then they walked 'round the corner,
To a whopping surprise!

The first time she saw him,
Ann thought, "What a clown,"
The man's selling Christmas trees,
That were grown upside down.

The girl said to her mother,
"Those trees can't be true,
They were grown upside down,
And they're red, white, and blue.

Ann walked on the tree lot,
And she touched the odd trees,
"May we ask what they cost,
May we ask Mother, please?"

So they asked the young man,
What it would cost them to buy,
A tree that was fat,
And at least eight feet high.

"Well," said the salesman,
"We have just such a tree,
Its shape is just perfect,
It cost ten, eighty three."

So Ann turned to her mother,
"May we buy it?" she cried,
"Let me think for a moment,"
Her mother replied.

"Well, we could," said her Mother,
"But how hard would it be?
To hang decorations,
On an upside down tree?"

"If we buy it," Ann said,
"I'll know just what to do,"
So they bought the tall tree,
And some mistletoe too.

A Wonderful Purchase

And they took it right home,
Little Ann was so glad,
She thought, "What a surprise,
I will have for my Dad."

And her Dad was surprised,
He said, "Oh my, what a sight,
An upside down Christmas tree,
That's red, blue, and white."

16

"Let's decorate" the girl said,
With a smile on her face,
So excited she was jumping,
All over the place.

"But how?" asked her Father,
"This tree's upside down,"
As he stared at the tree,
His smile turned to a frown.

18

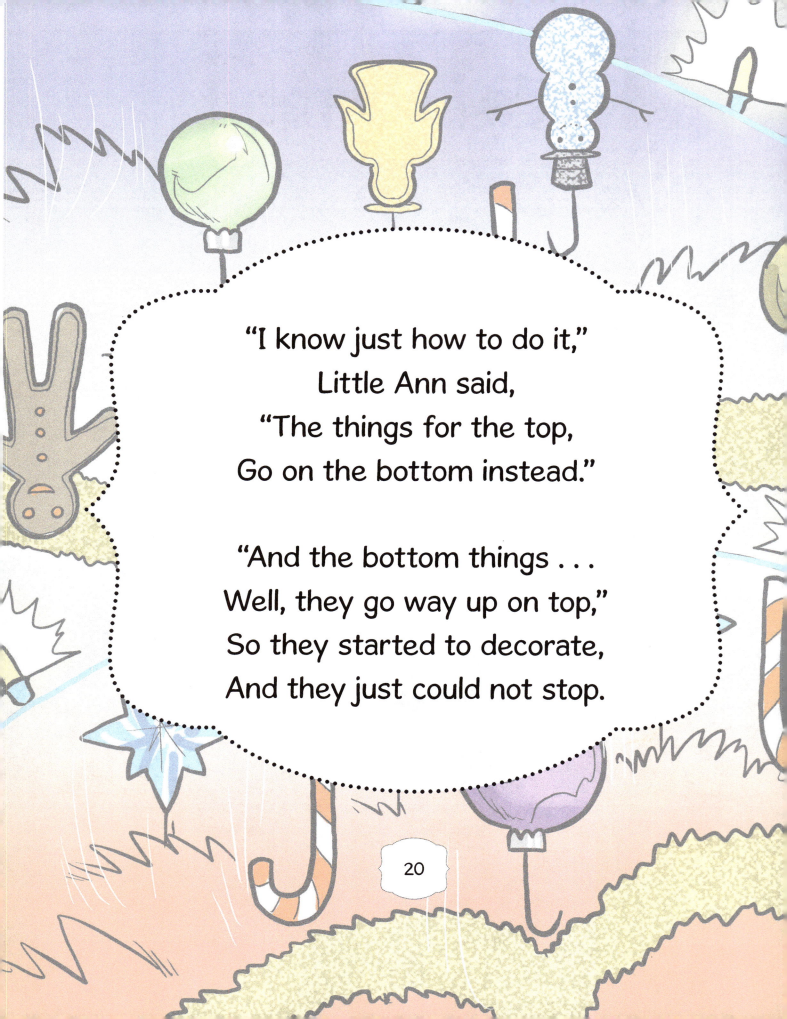

"I know just how to do it,"
Little Ann said,
"The things for the top,
Go on the bottom instead."

"And the bottom things . . .
Well, they go way up on top,"
So they started to decorate,
And they just could not stop.

Until later that evening,
Dad turned the lights low,
Then clicked on the tree lights,
Which started to glow.

It was immense and fantastic,
A beautiful sight!
The upside down Christmas tree,
Really sparkled that night.

On the floor was a manger,
With Joseph and Mary,
And wise men from the East,
With the gifts they could carry.

And, of course, baby Jesus,
Was asleep on the hay,
With animals all around him,
Quietly snoozing away.

On the tree Ann put candy canes,
And a big Santa Claus,
Silver, sparkly icicles,
Gold, white, and green balls.

There were snowmen and angels,
And bells that were red,
"I just love it, I love it!"
The little girl said.

A Beautiful Tree

They hung special decorations,
Ann had made all alone,
Using gold colored ribbon,
On a Styrofoam cone.

They added popcorn and cranberries,
And gingerbread men,
"It's the best in the world,"
Ann said with a grin.

"We love it too,"
Said the Dad with a smile,
"Let's all sit together,
And admire it awhile."

So they sat down all cozy,
With a warm Christmas feeling,
Admiring their odd tree,
That reached clear to the ceiling.

Then little Ann suggested,
How fantastic it would be,
To celebrate and honor,
Baby Jesus, and their tree.

So they made some hot chocolate,
And Mom started to bake,
Ann's enormously, all-time favorite,
Pineapple upside down cake.

A Fantastic Cake

The tree stood there gleaming,
Very sparkly and bright,
As if to say "Merry Christmas,"
To Ann's family that night.

34

So if you're out shopping,
And you happen to see,
A red, white, and blue thing,
Like an upside down tree.

Then buy one. And quickly.
Bring it home with good cheer.
May it bring you a Merry Christmas,
And a Happy New Year!

36

About the Author

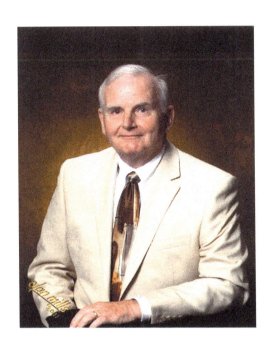

Charles (Richard) Esther's initial career path (and his undergraduate degree) was geared toward elementary education. However, after his U.S. Army service he chose to pursue a career with a educationally-oriented corporation where he rose to the position of director and stayed for 34 years. Throughout his life he has taught in Christian Education programs at every age level. Upon retirement he also served as a substitute teacher. Charles and his wife Donna are the parents of three grown children and ten fantastic grandchildren. This book was written for their young children many years ago. Married for almost 50 years they live on a small farm in the beautiful Shenandoah Valley of Virginia. This book is dedicated to my incredible wife, children and grandchildren.